SUMO BOY

BY Hirotaka Nakagawa

ILLUSTRATED BY Yoshifumi Hasegawa

HYPERION BOOKS FOR CHILDREN NEW YORK

Printed in Singapore
First U.S. Edition, 2006
1 3 5 7 9 10 8 6 4 2
Library of Congress Cataloging-in-Publication Data on file.
Reinforced binding
ISBN 0-7868-3635-0
This book is set in Cafeteria Regular.

Visit www.hyperionbooksforchildren.com

I am Sumo Boy.
I fight for justice.

"Sumo Boy, help!"

Uh-oh, somebody's in trouble.

"You bully—stop picking on that little girl."
"Drat, it's Sumo Boy."
"Take that!"
"Arrgh, salt!"

"Everything's okay now, little girl.
Are you hurt?"
"No, but I am hungry."

"Hi, I'm back!"
"Goodness, that must have been
quite a fight! Come and eat."

"Thank you, Sumo Boy.
Good-bye!"

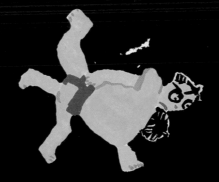

A note of explanation on the terms in the book

In sumo wrestling, **salt** is used for the ritual of purification and protection.

Dosukoi! is a traditional sumo battle cry.

Dojo is the name of the place where sumo wrestlers train.

Sumo hot pot is a traditional Japanese meal that sumo wrestlers eat, which is usually made of chicken, seafood, and vegetables in broth.

For more winning moves . . .

Frontal thrust-out

Frontal thrust-down

Frontal push-down

Frontal push-out

Frontal force-out

Headlock throw

Frontal crush-out

Backward force-down

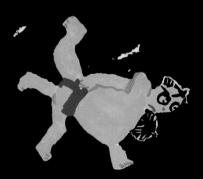

Pulling underarm throw

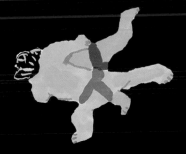

Overarm throw

Beltless arm throw-down

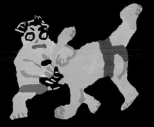

Under-shoulder swing

Pulling overarm throw

Outside leg trip

One-arm shoulder throw

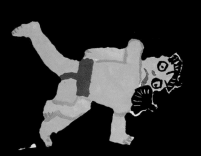

Body drop throw

Hooking backward counterthrow

Triple-attack force-out

Rear foot-sweep

Thigh scooping body drop

Leg pick

Reverse backward body drop

Backward body drop

Bell hammer backward body drop

Thrust-down

Arm bar counterthrow

Arm bar throw

Inner thigh-propping twist-down

Twisting underarm throw

Clasped-hands twist-down

Forward force-down

Lift-out

Backward belt throw

Rear push-down

Forward step-out

Backward pivot throw